Love, the moon & the stars between

Hannah Comrie

love, the moon & the stars between

love, the moon & the stars between
By Hannah Comrie

Copyright © 2021 Hannah Comrie
Paperback ISBN: 9798525086586

First edition published August 2021
Printed in Great Britain by Amazon

hannah comrie

Content, book & cover design, illustrations, typesetting and manuscript editing by Hannah Comrie.

Copyright © 2021 Hannah Comrie

All rights reserved. No part of this book may be reproduced without the written permission of the copyright owner except from quotations or passages in a review or reposted with credit to the author.

For more information, email **hcomrie24@gmail.com**

love, the moon & the stars between

hannah comrie

this book is for the boys who broke my heart
and i theirs

for the friends ive lost
and the ones ive found

for my friends & my family,
who believed in me before i did
i love you

love, the moon & the stars between

hannah comrie

dear reader

welcome to *love, the moon & the stars between*

my emotions, my hurt, my experience

love is ugly
love is brutal
love is what keeps me up at night

love is not perfect and therefore neither is this book

read with caution and care

love always

hannah comrie

love, the moon & the stars between

in these pages i present you my soul

hannah comrie

content note

this book includes sensitive material
including

…self-hatred
…eating disorders
…toxic relationships
…mental health
& more

please take care and look after yourself

love, the moon & the stars between

hannah comrie

contents

...the self
...the broken
...the damaged
...the hopeful
...the mended

love, the moon & the stars between

hannah comrie

the self

love, the moon & the stars between

i was the girl who hid under a wooden blanket
from the monsters in my wardrobe
who escaped
and couldnt leave me alone

hannah comrie

they ask me why i am so loud
i laugh
but truly i
am
afraid to be silenced
keep turning the volume up

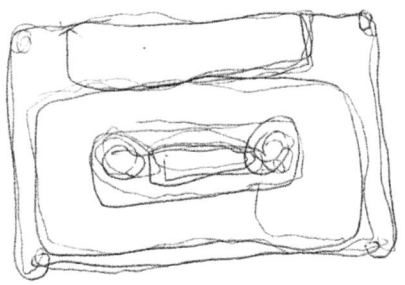

it is harder to be forgotten when you are easily heard

love, the moon & the stars between

the bands i adore
bore my heart
the words
and feelings
i found hard to feel

hannah comrie

sweet smiles and lovely words
masking nothing
but my hopeless wishes
that will never come true

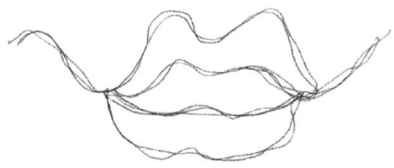

shit changes when you grow up

love, the moon & the stars between

my reflection taunts me
exposing the secrets of my fears
laughing at me

hannah comrie

i wonder if i'll ever get to feel like me again

love, the moon & the stars between

in the end false validation
is still
validation

hannah comrie

you consumed me before i got the chance to stop you
i still remember the smell
of half eaten food
taunting my mind

love, the moon & the stars between

i'm sorry i could not fix you
but glue does not work on a shattered heart

hannah comrie

i took comfort in pages of books
the escapism
from reality
and my tainted feelings
of you
and the world around us

love, the moon & the stars between

i wish that i had loved you better

a note to my younger self

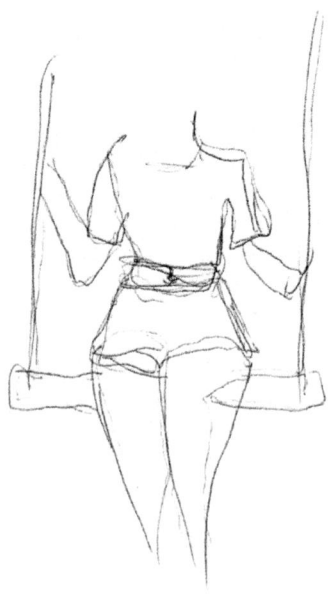

hannah comrie

they say my high expectations came from storybooks and
film screenings

and they are right

to an extent

as
they come from my mum
&
my dad
and the love they have for each other

love, the moon & the stars between

it didn't take too long to realise the toxic friendships began
long ago
during the lunchtimes
when
just us two
wanted to play

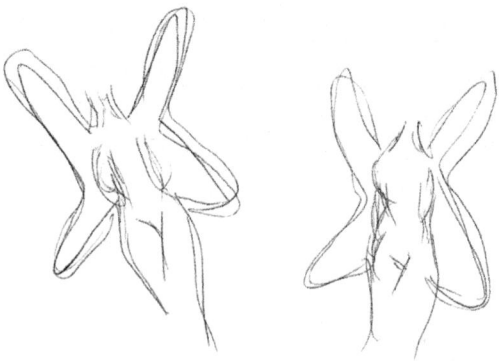

hannah comrie

they were blue
so i became blue
how silly of me to overlook the yellow

love, the moon & the stars between

i close my eyes and i am in a box
a box of my own torment
manipulation of the mind i can't silence

hannah comrie

for all the support i received, yours was the only i wanted
and you declined
uninterested and cruel

love, the moon & the stars between

the authors who i look up to will never understand
how they shaped me
took my hand
and led me out the darkness
to the light
showcasing who i truly am

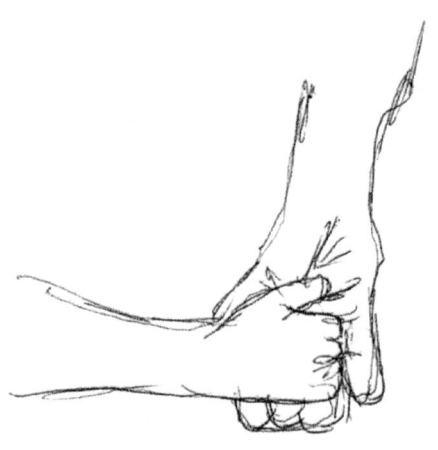

hannah comrie

the broken

love, the moon & the stars between

i should have told you i loved you
before you grew tired of waiting
i denied you
denied us
all because of foolish teenage pride

hannah comrie

it doesn't matter how much i try to lie to myself
i am in love
with you
and perhaps i always will be

regardless
you can never know
and we can never be together

love, the moon & the stars between

before the last glass is poured

before the last sip falls down your throat

remember all the times we should have had

before you picked up another bottle

hannah comrie

before

before

remember

before

love, the moon & the stars between

i made a playlist for you

of all the songs we used to scream in the car
the songs you once told me reminded you

of me

in five hours and thirty minutes i poured out my soul
lay it on the silver platter at your feet
waiting
to tell you my truth

but then you found her
and the playlist got shoved away
along with my feelings for you

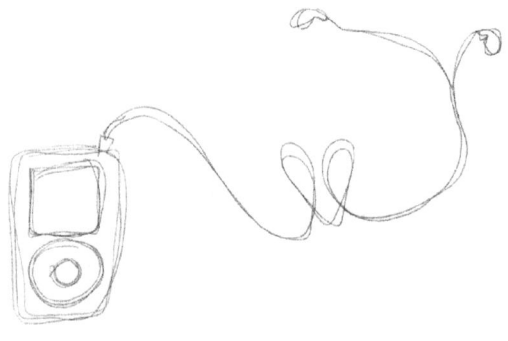

hannah comrie

i can't listen to that song anymore without thinking of you

Heartbroken (ft. you)

love, the moon & the stars between

i wish i could turn my feelings off and live life in control of my own emotions

hannah comrie

we were supposed to have the happy ending
not the twisted tragedy that fell upon us

love, the moon & the stars between

i am so sorry that my love for you was so much of a burden

hannah comrie

too many times we have pushed our friendship to be something more
maybe we will be better off friends
you once said to me

you will never lose me

i hope you meant it

please tell me you meant it

love, the moon & the stars between

i still read through our old messages
listen to the voice notes you sent
and i cry
over the love we once had
together
two souls torn apart time and again
only to be sewn together
and ripped by the seams
love lost in the needle of her

hannah comrie

when i sit on the floor of my shower blasting the music on my phone
i no longer think of you
your hands

&

the way they held me
the way the skin around your eyes would crinkle when you laughed
how everyone swore we would always be together

love, the moon & the stars between

everything we planned

it feels so long ago now
that we are as close as two strangers

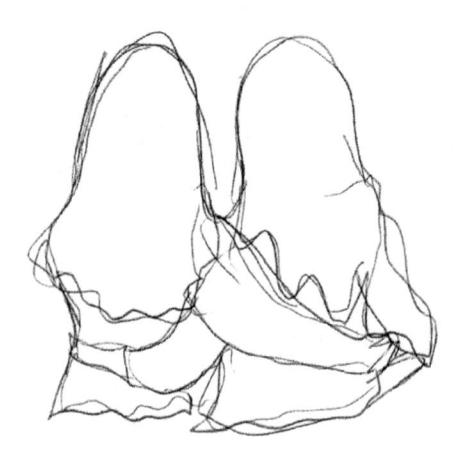

hannah comrie

i suppose things were never going to end well
as hard as we tried we were never going to be them
never going to understand the kind of love we wanted

love, the moon & the stars between

they tricked us
into thinking everything would be alright
that we would magically have everything fixed

hannah comrie

i spent years trying to find a way to make you love me
reaching for any sign of emotion
to fall from your pretty little head

love, the moon & the stars between

only phantoms of our characters remained
forgotten in the outtakes
of you and i
and the love we
were supposed to be
and lost

hannah comrie

please don't go
please stay

love, the moon & the stars between

the messages we sent lay dormant in your phone
decorating your inbox until you swiped left

the calls at night fell silent
when neither of us had anything left to say

all i wanted to hear was that we would be okay

hannah comrie

you only saw the rubble
rubbish in your eyes
abandoning it, moving on
shoveled into the bin at your disposal

but i wanted you to stay
to rebuild
reconstruct the rubble and begin again

love, the moon & the stars between

i tried to cut you out
to loosen the ties we had
but it became easier and easier to pick up your call

hannah comrie

you promised me forever
another pinky broken

you lied to me

love, the moon & the stars between

a loaded message

a trigger finger

and the things we should have kept to ourselves

hannah comrie

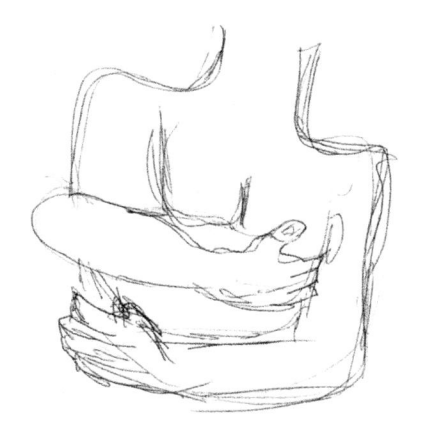

we are young

you whispered

life owes us no such thing as love

love, the moon & the stars between

as i called you
to not give up on me
you ignored the voicemail
and found volume in another

hannah comrie

i am still searching for the kindness in your voice that you
once promised me
all i feel are the abrasive walls
you built around your heart

love, the moon & the stars between

no amount of fairy lights
could ever
brighten
the darkness you left

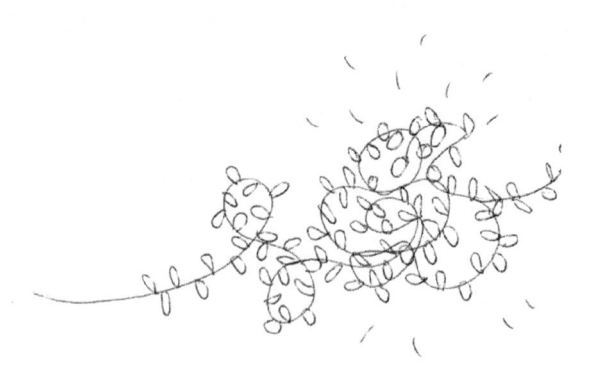

hannah comrie

this is not the love story we had hoped for
for this was not love at all

only salt claiming it was sugar
and two kids hiding in their broken home

love, the moon & the stars between

you told me i reminded you of a dream you had when you were younger,
i smiled because you

you were the nightmare that kept me up

hannah comrie

you made me believe i was my own worst enemy
that i was broken
tainted

love, the moon & the stars between

some people get roses and chocolates
i got phone calls at 3 am telling me all the things
i needed to do better

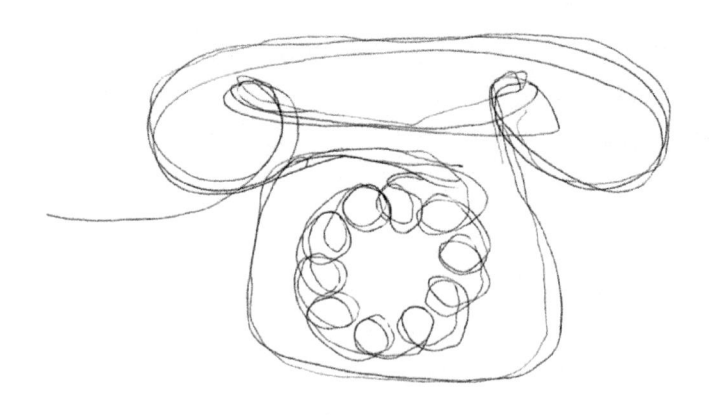

hannah comrie

beside the bitter cool wind
we told ourselves
its all just a load of astrological bullshit anyway

how the stars could define us
we never really knew

the way we would collide
and spark a disaster or two

we were just happy and in love
thanking our lucky stars up above

but that's all over now
together no more
only

star signs and snowflakes

with no where to go.

love, the moon & the stars between

i can't smile in pictures without being reminded of the
cruel things you would say about me behind my back
while you grinned at my heart

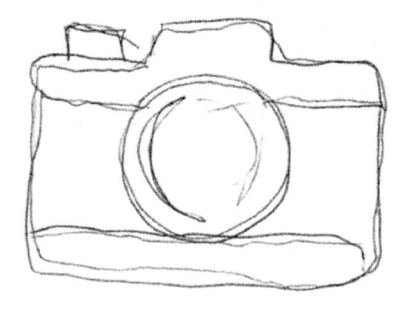

hannah comrie

the music stays loud so the thoughts that swarm my mind can be silenced

love, the moon & the stars between

did you enjoy the feel of my blood on your fingers when
you ripped my heart from my chest?

hannah comrie

i wish you would kiss me like you used to before you left me

love, the moon & the stars between

i screamed for help
but you didn't listen

hannah comrie

the damaged

love, the moon & the stars between

i spend my life
searching for a love like the stories on my shelf
for you to present yourself as a lost page

hannah comrie

i can't trust people who are too kind to me because you
made me believe everyone had an ultimatum hiding
behind their kind eyes

love, the moon & the stars between

you ask me why i am so clingy
i can't help it, i say
i'm used to being left behind

hannah comrie

prophecy and peace
the invoking of a future was lost
any sparks distilled by the rain
washing down your face
peppering kisses where i once had

love, the moon & the stars between

i envy your duvet
the way you wrap it around you
a warmth
comfort
the place you forget your troubles
plump pockets of peace
protecting you from the illness of the world

protection you once sought from me

hannah comrie

the moment you
stop treating yourself as an option
is the moment others do too

love, the moon & the stars between

*you became my moon
the light in the dark*

*the storm i never saw coming
the lightning, the rain*

*an ocean of starlight
 a cloud of...*

the morning you left
the day we fell apart

my soul felt crushed
as did my heart

hannah comrie

do you ever sit and think about us?
laying in the darkness of the night,
the stars around being your only light.
breathing in same air we did.

i ask you this because i do

sometimes the whistle of the wind reminds me of your smile
the sharp sound of your laugh cutting through the air
only leaving phantoms of the laughter that once was shared

love, the moon & the stars between

its magical
how the memory of us haunts me
yet yours lays forgotten in the graveyard of your teenage soul

hannah comrie

faint whispers became sirens
clouding the air with their voices

it became apparent that the stars in your eyes were brighter
than the speckles in the sky
the ties between you and i growing tighter

tighter

until the skin swell

love, the moon & the stars between

seeing me with him
happy
broke you didn't it

it broke me too

hannah comrie

> the part you wanted
> didn't want me

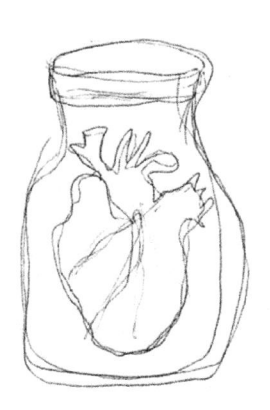

love, the moon & the stars between

before you love her
before you leave me

remember every part of me tried

hannah comrie

if you need to beg them to stay they will find another
reason to leave
you are worth staying for
let them go

love, the moon & the stars between

it doesn't matter what you do in life, there are always going to be people who trample on your happiness, just make sure you build them a bridge to help them find their way home

hannah comrie

we were picking daisies

happy in our own little world before a thorn emerged
tainting your attention
prickling us both

the only reminder of us being
scars under your fingertips

i don't like daisies anymore

love, the moon & the stars between

she was the beginning of our end

the sunlight in your storm
paving the way for it

maybe in another life, another world, another time
you would be mine

hannah comrie

i wished for starlight
but

it poured
the rain drowning out my thoughts of you

it didn't matter that you were my umbrella
because i wasn't yours

so like a butterfly
i let you go

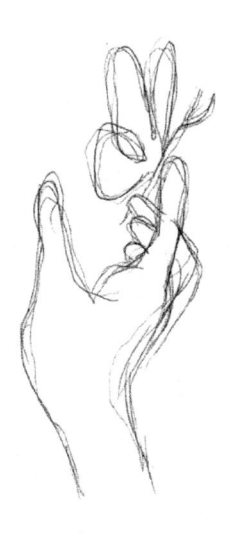

love, the moon & the stars between

to be addicted to you would be something id happily go to therapy for

hannah comrie

she isnt someone who you should love,

she is someone you would walk past in the street,
wondering why her smile lay dormant
awaiting an earthquake, a fault line
so she could finally erupt

her heart caged by bulletproof glass, your hand on the trigger ready to pull
she was not the person she once was, only a shadow of her former self

yet you admired the darkness, a beaconing light allowing
for her to be shown

she was tough and you loved her

you still do

love, the moon & the stars between

they say im a dreamer

& i will always dream of a life where you loved me
where you didn't let me go

hannah comrie

the hardest pill to swallow was realising that i may have
been yours
but you would never be mine
and im sorry i couldn't love you the way you wanted to be
loved

love, the moon & the stars between

you made all my fictional fantasies come true

the stories of love and lust
becoming overruled by the magic we created
i sometimes forget the memory of us wasn't entirely fictional
being shared on twitter by teenage romantics
hoping one day to find a love that we did

like all good books our story came to an end
the last page becoming lost in a sea of thoughts
of a sequel or two that was cut
laying flat on the floor of our old room

the memory of us on the shelf
squashed between romance and lost love
fragments of our past laying beside the dust
being stirred when either of us wants a re-read
until it settles again
creating a cocoon around the story of a love that was beautiful and tragic

between pages of teenage romance

hannah comrie

i should thank you
for pointing out the things in me you hated
which made me love them more

love, the moon & the stars between

i found it in the trees
the bees in the sky
i found a reason to stay
when you made me question why

hannah comrie

im turning off my phone to feel like me again

love, the moon & the stars between

stop trying to pretend what we had was love

hannah comrie

you told me we were a storybook love story
you just failed to mention there was no happy ending

love, the moon & the stars between

society is suffocating me
society is suffocating me
society is suffocating me
society is suffocating me
society is suffocating me

society
is
suffocating
me

hannah comrie

you kept saying
you needed me
and i believed you

love, the moon & the stars between

i wish it was all just a nightmare and you would have left me alone
but the memory of us dancing in the street is only but a dream in my mind

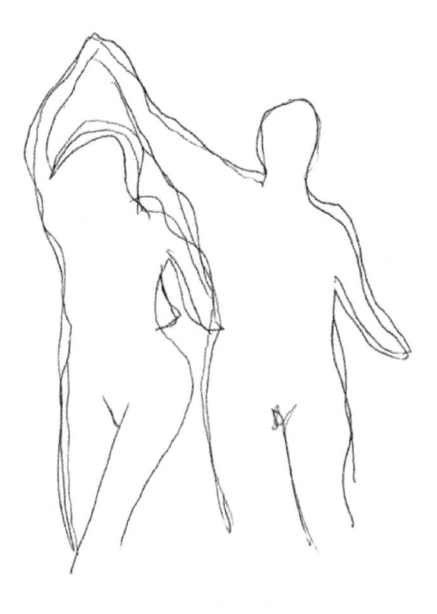

hannah comrie

fictional worlds are a lot less cruel than this one honey

love, the moon & the stars between

i wish i never met you

hannah comrie

the hopeful

love, the moon & the stars between

i am but the twinkle you get in your eye when you think of
us
the things we are
to each other
and ourselves

hannah comrie

forgiveness lies in your fingertips
dancing along the screen
painting pretty pictures of us from before

captivating my very soul

love, the moon & the stars between

the girl you hurt isn't me anymore
she came through the thunderstorm
her own umbrella
she grew up and sought the sunshine

hannah comrie

the likeness in your smile makes my heart
flutter
like the three bees you keep on your arm

permanent

love, the moon & the stars between

you made me believe in myself again
when i felt that i had no hope
no future
you molded me into the person i am
and the person i am to become

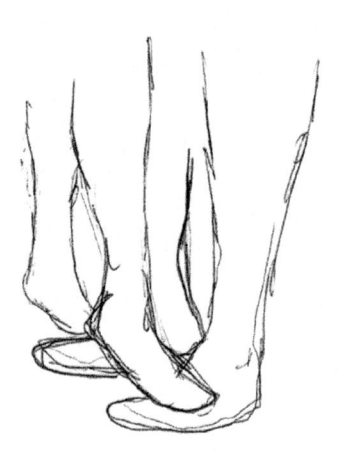

hannah comrie

silly boys do not control my feelings
silly boys do not control my feelings
silly boys do not control my feelings
silly boys do not control my feelings

anymore

love, the moon & the stars between

you tried to wash me away
but i kept on fighting
&

i won't stop

hannah comrie

to think i once let an asshole like you dictate my feelings
its funny
you truly believe i still care about you
who is the fool now darling?

love, the moon & the stars between

i'm used to finding myself with too much to say but you make me speechless

hannah comrie

how do i convey to you that you bear my heart?

love, the moon & the stars between

i hate that you make me feel the things i once believed to be fictional

hannah comrie

dandelions whisper to me
they sing their sweet song
of kindness and of sorrow
of their hope
for another tomorrow

love, the moon & the stars between

like a constellation of stars my feelings of myself change according to a calendar i keep on myself

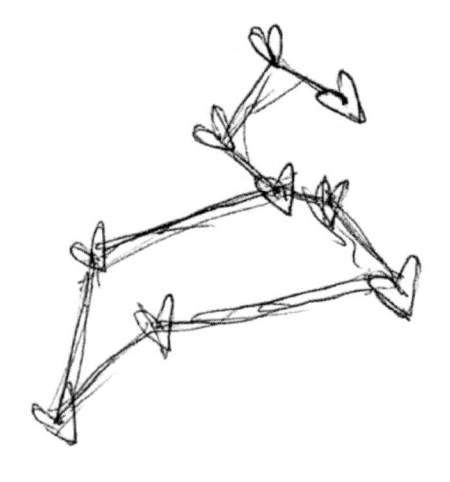

hannah comrie

the mended

love, the moon & the stars between

i recall one thing my mother told me

beware the stare of broken boys
for they will capture you, lock you up with their forgotten toys

they will try to be better
sometimes you wont be able to tell.
they will shout, they will pry
and sometimes they may even make you cry

after everything i never thought i would love again
i felt hopeless
like as though i was the broken boy

but

one day a broken boy may need a little glue
to fix the wounds, mend them up like new
if they are lucky and try very hard
that same broken boy may be loved by a girl like you

you taught me to feel
what it meant to be loved and be in love
with you

hannah comrie

the day i decided to love myself was the day i said
fuck you to society
and began to live for me

love, the moon & the stars between

in the car we paused
as your heartbeat echoed my own

hannah comrie

i am my own semi colon

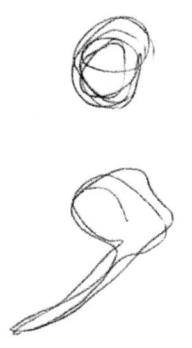

love, the moon & the stars between

you ask me what is trust?

trust is knowing aphrodite herself looks at you for love

& that is why i love you

for not your beauty nor body

but your soul

and how you love mine
and keep your eyes on me

for even a greek goddess will not make your hands wander

hannah comrie

sometimes i look at you, in the shadow of the headlights

and stare

for every star in the sky
will forever endeavor to shine
as bright as your smile

love, the moon & the stars between

love is not romance
love is not friendship
love is life
and to live is to love

and to love you is a life of eternity

hannah comrie

before

i would cling for validation in the form of likes

now i have learned that to love one's self is enough for me

love, the moon & the stars between

you ask me why i have been distant
leaving you delivered
i learned that we didn't work
& that *i* did

i've never been so happy

hannah comrie

listen to me closely
for i will only say this once
take a breath, listen to the song of the birds
a second, count to ten

you are only you for a lifetime

stop waiting for the moment and take it

love, the moon & the stars between

mirrors are no longer my enemy
they are my friend
displaying all the things i love
once again

hannah comrie

what if every negative thought i had about myself was just
a manifestation of you?

love, the moon & the stars between

the nights in the dark where we kept on driving
that is what i live for

hannah comrie

start dancing with yourself in your room

stop waiting for an excuse and dance with you

love, the moon & the stars between

for the lovers who find themselves clinging to the fantasies
in their head

don't wait forever babe
make them happen

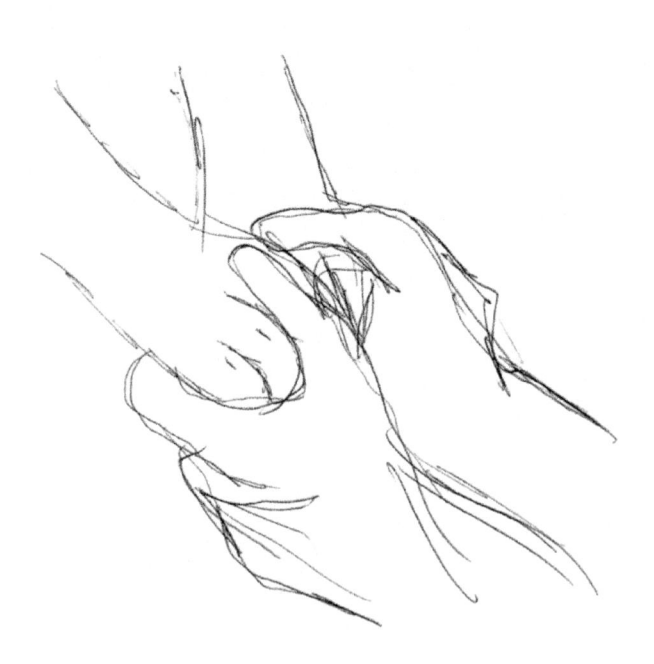

hannah comrie

thank you
for teaching me to love myself
again

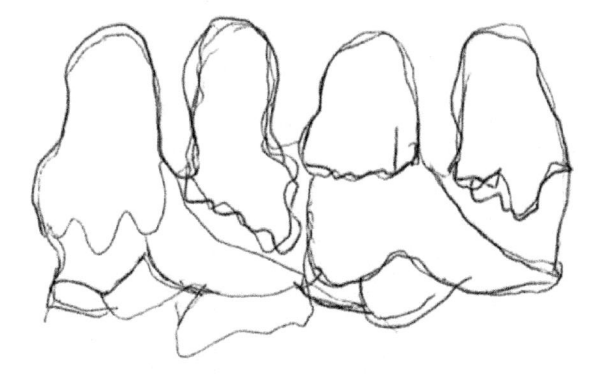

acknowledgements

thank you to my family, especially my mum and dad for reading my scribbles on paper and listening to me go on and on about this book i was going to write. thank you for believing i could do this, for pushing me to go for it.

thank you to aimee, lucy, grace & beth for lighting up my darkest moments. for listening to me cry at 2am and crying with me. thank you for standing by me and loving me.

thank you to my teachers & my lecturers who read my work before it was written, who pushed me to do better and keep on pushing. especially miss ainslie, for reading all the words i put before you and still doing it with a smile on your face.

hannah comrie

&
    thank you to

those of you who matter to me,

      who i love because

        you made this

           i may have been the writer but you were
the heart

           that filled me with love

      when i felt deflated and empty

love, the moon & the stars between

Connect with the author

Instagram: @hannahcomriex
Twitter: @hannah_comrie
Website: www.hannahcomrie.com
Email: hcomrie24@gmail.com

hannah comrie

thank you for taking the time to read *love, the moon & the stars between*

volume two is already in the making….

love, the moon & the stars between

hannah comrie